For the rest of the Carter family—Alice, Noah, and Finlay x

American edition published in 2019 by Andersen Press USA,
an imprint of Andersen Press Ltd.
www.andersenpressusa.com

First published in Great Britain in 2019 by Andersen Press Ltd.,
20 Vauxhall Bridge Road, London SW1V 2SA.
Copyright © Graham Carter, 2019

Distributed in the United States and Canada by
Lerner Publishing Group, Inc.
241 First Avenue North
Minneapolis, MN 55401 USA
For reading levels and more
information, look up this title at
www.lernerbooks.com.

Printed and bound in China.

Library of Congress Cataloging-in-Publication Data Available
ISBN: 978-1-5415-7762-6
eBook ISBN: 978-1-5415-7769-5
1-TOPPAN-6/1/19

Graham Carter

OTTO BLOTTER

Bird Spotter

Andersen Press USA

Turtledove was a town much like any other,
except for one small difference ...

it was FULL of birds and bird-spotters.

And the most famous
spotters were a family
named Blotter.

The Blotters spent every moment of every day spotting birds.

They'd even turned their home into the perfect bird blind
so they NEVER had to leave it.

But young Otto Blotter was NOT a spotter!

He didn't like staying indoors all day.

What he liked was to EXPLORE!

On this particular day,
Otto made an extraordinary
discovery . . .

That's a huge footprint!

Hidden in the bushes,
all alone, sat the most
unusual little BIRD.

Otto wasn't allowed to keep pets, but he couldn't just leave the little fellow.
He scooped up Bird and sneaked him back to his room.
Luckily his family was too busy to notice.

The next day, Otto took his feathery
friend to all his favorite
exploring spots.

And sneakily fed and bathed
him after the rest of the
family had gone to bed.

TUESDAY

MONDAY

WEDNESDAY

But as the days passed,
Otto started to
notice some BIG
changes . . .

THURSDAY

SATURDAY

FRIDAY

His little friend was not so little anymore.

And Otto's secret was becoming TOO BIG to hide.

Otto knew Bird was going to be
discovered any minute.
There was nothing more he could do
to hide his huge friend!

Luckily, Bird didn't like to see Otto upset. He knew this was the moment to show his friend something truly remarkable . . .

Good day Otto!

CAMOUFLAGE!

Otto was over the moon!

Bird could disguise
himself as anything.
It meant they could
go anywhere.

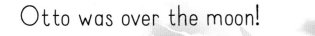

They could once again visit their favorite spots and go on fabulous adventures.

And no one would ever know.

Otto and Bird could not have been happier, until the day they visited the zoo.

As they passed family after family of meerkats, penguins,

monkeys, and stingrays, Bird seemed to grow sadder and sadder.

Otto's thoughts flashed back to the day he first found Bird:
the huge footprints, the giant feathers, the massive pile of poo . . .

Suddenly he realized:
Bird hadn't been alone.
Bird had a family!

But Otto was going to need help to find them.

After recovering from meeting the most majestic bird ever discovered,
the whole Blotter family set to work helping Otto come up with a plan.

By nightfall they had made the tallest bird-spotting tower ever built.
The Blotters were sure they would spot Bird's family in no time now.

They peered for hours and hours into the still, inky night, but they didn't spot a thing. "Don't worry Bird," said Otto. "We WILL find your family."

FUM-EE?

FAAM-EE?

FAAAAM-LEE?

Then something
magical happened.
"FAMILY!" cried Bird,

glowing
so brightly,
he lit up the
whole night.

In the distance, something began to rustle … something began to stir …

and something began to glow. One by one, three even bigger birds

came out of the darkness. They'd found them!

Otto was really happy
that his friend had
found his family.

But that didn't make it any easier when the time came to say goodbye.

The Blotters hoped they
would spot him again one day though.

After all—they were experts.

From that day on, Otto became a top spotter himself.

And the rest of the Blotters found that
exploring with Otto led to all kinds of amazing
discoveries (and the odd adventure).